SOMETHING RIGHT

A TALE OF THE DEVARIAN DRAGON REALM

JENNI WARD

MIRAWORTH BOOKS

First published in 2022
This edition by Miraworth Books
ABN 44 964 848 123

MIRAWORTH BOOKS
PO Box 3523, Mount Gambier, SA 5290, Australia

ISBN (e-book): 978-0-6453270-7-6
ISBN (paperback): 978-0-6453270-8-3

Originally published as part of the Adamant Spirits: 2022 Charity Anthology

Cover design by Andrea Fodor of CReya-tive

CHAPTER 1

I TAPPED MY pencil against the fabric case. The professor had kicked a girl out of the class the previous week when she dared to tap her pen on the desk. Still, the rhythmic beat helped me to think about the presentation.

Mythical Creatures Philosophy wasn't exactly a subject I needed to take, but the idea of creatures that might have once existed–maybe still exist somewhere remote–fascinated me.

1

My gaze wandered around the room. A lot of people had taken the course, but now, three weeks in, the numbers had dwindled as the withdrawal date passed. I suspected a few were only here to grab an easy grade. I skipped my gaze back a couple of rows and had to turn my head to see Marc.

Marc stared straight ahead at the professor; he used to do the same back in high school as well. I had believed he had been super focused, but he'd never made the top of the class lists. As I stared at him, he looked my way. Our eyes met for a moment and I felt the instant connection I always did. Still, I diverted my attention back to the front of the room. The professor had his back turned to the class as he talked about the theory behind dragons, perhaps an extinct lizard species.

I watched as the screen changed to show a map, segmented by colours over certain countries. Smaller images appeared, showing the different dragons that appeared in mythology and linked them to the source areas. I had been given a book once for a birthday about dragon species. The illustrations had fascinated me.

Perhaps that's why the professor hadn't held my attention, and I dared to sneak another glance over my shoulder at Marc. His attention seemed fully on the presentation. I should have pulled out of the class the moment I saw him there on day one. I had spent the better part of high school hoping to catch his eye, hoping that he felt that same connection I did whenever we were close.

There wasn't anything in particular about Marc that set him apart from the other guys in the room. His black hair fell loose around his face and sometimes, when the light was right, it looked like he had silver streaks through it. He had been the only guy I had dressed up for last year for the end-of-year social and after all my effort he hadn't even attended. I had tried not to take it personally. From what I've seen, he'd never shown an interest in going out with any particular girl. As I watched him from where I sat, I couldn't help but feel drawn to him again. As if something deep inside of me wanted to know him as well as I knew myself.

Before the thought had left my mind, it happened again. His head turned towards me and there was no glancing away. I mustered up a half smile and thought I saw the corner of his own mouth turn, but perhaps it was just a trick of the light.

I turned back to the professor and listened until the end of the session. As soon as he dismissed the class, chairs scraped on the floor and the mass of the people that remained headed for the two exits on either side. I picked up my books and turned around, hoping to see which way Marc had gone. I caught a glimmer of his black hair just as he exited the door and grabbed my bag to follow as quickly as I could.

The people in front of me weren't interested in moving fast. Well, not as fast as I wanted them to move. I wasn't that keen on the night classes as it was, but I had to work around the part-time job I'd gotten to try to pay towards my fees. When people finally moved out of my way, I made my way down the corridor and out the main door, where I hoped Marc had headed.

Outside of the door, I pulled my jacket around me tighter. I stood still for a moment as my breath played in the air. People walked around me as I searched for him. I knew that I should have just gone straight to my car. It was a sensible thing to do. It was what they would expect me to do. I stood there glancing around the landscaped section at the front of the uni, trying to discern something in the darkness.

Above me the full moon sat against a clear backdrop of stars. There was no warmth at all. I heard a cry rise from my side and I turned my head towards it.

I felt pulled towards the cry and my shoes hit every second step. On the pavement, I followed the pull down towards a group of trees where shadows lurked beneath, where light didn't reach. I was still a little distance away, but my eyes could discern at least three figures.

"I don't want any trouble." Marc. His even, calm tone was recognisable.

"Who says that you have a choice in the matter, mate? Your brother is a difficult one to track down. Now, you gonna do this the easy way or the hard way?" a vaguely unfamiliar male voice asked.

I cursed myself for wearing heels tonight, of all nights. They clacked against the pavement as I drew closer, even though I tried to keep on the balls of my feet.

One shadow turned and stepped towards me, stopping at the edge of the tree's shadow.

"She's got nothing to do with this," Marc said, his head turned in my direction.

The figure left the anonymity of the shadows as the moon highlighted his features. I recognised him from high school: Jacob. He'd been a senior leader, captain of the football team, and somehow got a high score on the final exams. Still, brains didn't mean he wasn't an idiot. A sneer appeared on Jacob's face as he gave me a once-over chilled me; he hadn't changed at all; once a creep, always a creep.

"What's going on?" I asked, trying to see past him to the two remaining shadows.

"Nothing that needs to bother you. How about I walk into your car?" He extended a hand towards me and I paused.

"Hope you don't mind if I pass on that. I think I'm safer without your help, to be honest."

"Always had a mouth on you, haven't you, Belle?" Jacob glanced over his shoulder.

"Since when is being assertive having a mouth? I have brothers who are very protective of me, but they made me earn my place in the family. So how about you to just back off and let us get on with our evening?"

"Belle, just go," Marc said.

"Not until I know these two guys are going as well." I was determined to stand my ground.

"We're not fussy. I would have taken Marc's phone, maybe the shoes if they were a good brand... but maybe there is something I can take from you as well," Jacob said, and he pulled out a knife from his pocket.

I hesitated as the steel glinted in the night. The toes of my shoe dug into the ground as I focused on Marc beneath the tree's canopy. I raised my hands up in defence but it was probably too late to play the helpless female card.

"Leave her be." Marc's usual neutral tone had a sharp warning to it.

"And who's gonna make me, Marc? You can't even keep your little brother in line, let alone anyone else."

Jacob made his move and reached out for my arm. I turned, but not fast enough as his fingers curled around me. I kicked my foot back and connected with his knee. The move didn't set me free. My other hand reached out and grabbed his wrist as the knife moved closer to my face. I used all my strength to keep it at bay. My mind raced as I tried to remember the moves that my eldest brother had taught me after his judo lessons, but my mind wouldn't cooperate.

"This is going to be more fun than I thought," he hissed. My ear felt the heat of his breath.

I heard a cry of pain somewhere behind me. He attempted to move the knife. I pushed against his arm. I swallowed hard. Fighting one guy came with a set of issues. If I had to deal with both, I would be done for. He tightened his arm's hold around my neck and I struggled to take in air.

Heel. I slammed my shoe down hard; a direct hit. I heard him whimper as I twisted my foot as I pressed it down harder. His grip loosened a little from my neck.

"I said to leave her be!" Marc yelled.

Relief flooded me and I continued to keep my hold on the assailant's arm while digging my heel in as best I could. Jacob spun me around and I saw Marc a few steps away.

"What did you do to him?" The first sign of wavering that I'd heard in Jacob's voice.

"I said to leave her be."

The knife dropped from view as Jacob released me with a shove forward. I stumbled and held out my hands to brace for the impact, leaning to the side to land on the grass. On the ground, I rolled over in time to see Jacob had the knife directed at Marc. He jabbed the knife towards Marc, who stepped away. Then Marc moved forward, and the knife came down. Marc raised his arm in defence too late. He cried out in pain as steel cut through the jacket. A bright blue flash engulfed Marc first and then Jacob. It faded just as quickly. Jacob lay on the ground, eyes closed but his chest continued to rise and fall.

I allowed Jacob only the briefest of a glance. I watched Marc, unsure if I had seen what I thought I had. *Was it real? Surely I didn't. Nothing like that could be real.*

Marc leaned over and I could see the rapid breaths coursing from his mouth. His head turned to look at me and he straightened up.

"Come on, let's get you back to your car." He held out his hand.

I sat up and brushed my hands together. My gaze fell on his arm; the cut in the jacket was wet with what I assumed to be blood.

"What about your arm?"

He waved his hand. "Don't worry about that. I'll deal with it later."

I took his hand, and he pulled me to my feet. I tried to find my balance on the heels, but for some reason I couldn't seem to get it. When I looked down, I saw that the heel on the right shoe had completely snapped off: a lesson learnt about heels and running.

"Give me a second." Even as I said the words, I felt the warmth of his hand as it clasped mine.

It would have been easier and quicker to remove the shoes with two hands, but my hand refused to entertain the idea. I pushed my shoes off with my feet before I bent down to pick them up. Marc's grip hadn't wavered.

"Car park," he said, and I nodded.

We walked along the pavement in silence. A handful of students lingered in the car park chatting and saying their goodbyes. I wondered how we looked to them, probably no different. None of them seemed aware of what had just happened.

"This one yours?" he asked when I stopped beside a blue Mini.

"Yeah," I replied.

I felt the cool air on my hand again, but he didn't move away. I riffled through my bag, trying to find the car key. Several times my fingers brushed across them, but I fumbled it each time to retrieve them. On the umpteenth attempt, I finally grabbed hold of them and unlocked the car.

Marc stepped back as I opened the door and got into the driver's seat. I glanced up at him to see his gaze darting around the car before it fell back on me.

"No picking any fights with people who aren't your size for the rest of the night. Promise?"

I hesitated; I had the key in the ignition. All I had to do was smile and promise, right? "I saw something Marc, I swear I..."

"Go home, Belle. You're just tired." Marc pushed the car door closed and gave me a wave as he stepped back from the car.

I turned the key in the ignition; I wasn't convinced. I had seen something. He was watching me as I looked out the window. His skin looked normal. Marc waved a second time, and I reversed out of the park and headed out of the car park. I flicked on the blinker and looked in the rear-view mirror. He stood where my car had been, his hands in his jean pockets. Those scales had been as real as the jacket he wore.

CHAPTER 2

FOR TWO DAYS, I had looked for Marc on campus but saw no sign of him. My mind continued to replay the night, wondering if it had just been my imagination. In my mind, I saw Marc yell. A blue light emanated from his body as scales glinted on his hands, his neck and face. Then the light faded and there had been no sign of the scales on his arm.

Perhaps I had been too far away. I was tired. I walked down the corridor, in flats this time. Not a lot of students were on campus, as it was Friday. I glanced at the paper on top of my book. I needed to get that assignment done this weekend to save my sanity.

I passed the information counter and went to turn down the next corner to head towards the library.

"Sorry," I mumbled. I stepped back from the body I had bumped into.

"No worries."

I looked up to see a brief smile pass over Marc's face. My heart raced faster. My mind struggled to find the words to ask what I had wanted. I felt the book slipping and adjusted my arm. Too late. I moved my foot to prepare for the book, hitting the ground, but just the paper floated onto it.

Marc held the book in his hand. "Sorry, missed the paper."

"Wow, some reflex action," I replied. I bent down to pick up the paper. His jeans covered his legs to his shoes; there would be no way to see anything like scales there. The paper refused to be retrieved until the third try.

"Ta," I said and placed the paper back where it had been. "Hey, you wouldn't like to go for a coffee or something at the café, would you?"

The smile faded from his face and he looked beyond me before he stepped to move around me

"No, I can't... Sorry."

"Come on Marc, as a thank you." I watched as he paused. My eyes fell back to the paper. "We could go over the assignment for mythology class. It's just a coffee."

He turned his head towards me and I watched as his hair fell back against his face.

"Mythology assignment, huh?"

"I haven't had a chance to do it yet."

"You picked a topic yet?"

I nodded. "I was thinking of looking at the connection between dragons and the locations where the mythology is strongest."

He's going to say no. He reached up tucked his fringe behind his ear.

"Okay, sure."

The breath exited my mouth, and I filled my lungs again. A smile covered my face that I had difficulty tempering. He fell in beside me and we walked towards the university café located opposite the library.

My fingers gripped the bottom of the book tightly. I hadn't been on many dates, just enough to have the taste of it and know that my patience with small talk with some people wasn't that great.

When we arrived, the cafe was pretty much deserted. We took a seat near the window and I reluctantly put the book down. My hands felt sweaty from gripping them so tightly and I suddenly wiped them over my jeans.

"What do you think you might like to drink?" Marc asked. He pulled the seat out opposite to me.

"Um, maybe a hot chocolate would be nice?" I wondered if that was the correct answer, especially after I'd suggested a coffee. However, I hardly ever drank coffee, loved the scent, I just didn't like the taste.

"Sounds good."

Marc removed his black jacket and hooked it on the back of the chair. My gaze was drawn away from his face to his muscular upper arm that his singlet showed off. The dragon tattoo curled around in flying formation on his bicep.

"I'll go order."

I stood up quick enough that I misjudged the table and I rubbed my knee. "I invited you, remember? I really should be the one to go order and pay."

Marc did one of his little half-smiles again and shook his head. "I still owe you for the other night when you came to my rescue, remember?"

How can I forget? He turned and headed towards the counter. My cheeks warmed at the reference. Not wanting to feel like a coat stand, I sat on the chair, careful to avoid hitting my knee on the table leg as I swung them beneath the table.

Marc had moved just out of my sight. I turned my attention out the window. The view wasn't much more than a bunch of bushes, but it filled the moments before I heard his footsteps approach the table again. I turned my head in time to see him place the order number on the table.

Once seated, I searched my mind for something to say. Instead of the witty conversation I had imagined, an awkward silence descended over us. My hands rubbed against my jeans beneath the table as I glanced over at Marc. I reminded myself this wasn't a date, just a drink, nothing more than that.

"It's a little bit different from high school, isn't it?" Marc said.

I allowed the air to escape. *Had I been holding my breath? I can do this.*

"It is a bit, but I think I prefer it to high school."

"Yeah, me too. I do like being able to wear whatever I want rather than the uniform."

Can't complain about the view at the moment either. My cheeks burned at the thought.

"So, have you started the assignment, then?" I asked.

"I had been planning to do it this weekend," Marc paused and he fiddled with the stand of the order number. "Things have been a bit complicated at home. I've been trying to deal with some stuff and... I don't know… I've just found it hard to find the right headspace to get it done with Tim at home."

Tim. I could hardly forget him.

"Your younger brother." The words sounded flat, but I tried to keep the bitterness out. Somehow, whenever I had tried to talk to Marc in high school, Tim would show up.

"Yeah, you'd probably remember he was always a bit too headstrong for his own good. He likes to get his own way when he thinks he's right. I guess you get that. You have siblings too, right?"

"Yeah, four older brothers, but I don't think it's the same. I mean, you're the eldest and I'm the youngest, so it probably equates to a different experience. I'm more used to being told I can do stuff and then worried I'll fail. I kind of always felt like I had to be like them more than myself."

"I think you're fine the way you are."

"Thanks." My cheeks burned up again and my mouth twitched. "Well, you know, if we did the assignment together, I guess we could get it done quicker. The professor did say we could work in groups if we wanted to."

Marc raised his gaze from the table to me and smiled. "I think I've become so used to doing these assignments on my own, I never even considered teaming up. Man, like in high school, you'd be put in a group and you'd end up getting stuck doing all the work. Hang on."

Marc stood up and grabbed the back of his chair. He swung it around to the space at the side of the table. I angled my knees towards the wall to give him space for his legs under the table.

"Are these the notes you made about what you wanted to cover?" he asked as he reached out for my notebook.

"That's what I was thinking about."

Was thinking about... now my attention is on just how close you are and how much I wanted to accidentally reach out... I saw him open the notebook, but my gaze fell on the dragon tattoo again.

"Did it hurt getting that?"

Marc looked away from the paper and at me. *Shit, I said that aloud.* He reached his hand over his chest and ran his hand over the ink. "It wasn't without pain. I can tell you that much. But it wasn't too bad. It was actually my brother's idea."

"You must be really close if you were willing to get a tattoo like that."

"Worst of enemies, but the best of friends. Tim's got a matching one; I guess it helps us to feel that we are connected. We are not exactly flush with the same type of personality."

My gaze switched between his blue eyes and the lines of the dragon tattoo. I wanted to reach out and trace the ink with my finger. I clasped my hands in my lap to resist the temptation.

"Who knows, Belle, maybe one day you'll get a tattoo too."

A short laugh burst from my lips. "I don't know how well that would go down with the folks back home."

"I think you can take care of yourself."

The familiar warmth spread into my cheeks. When I glanced up, he had leaned forward, his eyes enticed me to move closer.

The clatter of a cup on a saucer distracted us both as the hot chocolate arrived. The connection broke even though the pull remained. I released my hands to pull one cup closer to me and noticed Marc had ordered the same.

The conversation that followed remained on the assignment at hand. I found it easy to chat about that topic without feeling like someone turned up the heat. After the third hot chocolate, the workers closed up the café for the day.

Outside, we walked to the car park. The air felt fresh as I breathed it in. When my car came into view, I slowed my pace. The moment had to end at some point, but I wanted any extra minutes I could grab.

Neither of us had said a word from the café to the car. The lights flashed when I pressed the button. I purposely opened the passenger door and placed my books and notebook on it. Before writing down my number, I ripped a piece of paper from the back page. I clenched the paper in my hand as I walked back around to the driver's side - where Marc stood, just as he had on that night.

"Maybe we can get together tomorrow and keep working on it," I suggested. Behind my back, I crossed my fingers.

"Yeah, we can work out something and do that. Maybe we could meet somewhere other than here," Marc replied. "Come on, better get you heading home before the rain starts."

"What rain?" I looked up at the sky; a few clouds marked the blue canvas, but nothing that indicated rain. "I think you're imagining the rain."

Marc reached around me and pulled on the door handle. "Trust me, if you go now, you might avoid the downpour."

He stepped a little closer, and his hand rested on the top the car. My fingers played with the piece of paper. *He's just waiting until I get into the car.* At that moment, he stood so close. His open jacket even rested against my body slightly. I felt pulled towards him again, an invisible string that tugged at me; it told me to move closer.

"Marc?"

"Yeah?" he replied. It sounded rather absent, but he looked down at me.

"Here." I placed the piece of paper into his empty hand. "And Marc?"

"Yeah?"

I bit my lip. *Now or never.*

"I just want to say, because I've wanted to say it for a really long time, that you really are the nicest guy I've ever known." I hesitated for a moment as I waited for a reaction. When he said nothing, I ventured to add, "Whatever it is you think you can't tell me, you can, whenever you're ready."

I moved closer and kissed him quickly on the lips. It lasted only a fraction of a second, but I felt a rush of tingling race through my body from my lips to my toes. I turned and sat down in the driver's seat. I wasn't sure if I pulled on the door or if he closed it. My gaze focused through the windscreen as I backed out of the park. Then I did it. I looked at Marc and gave him a small wave. My heart raced, and a smile crept across my face as he raised his hand in response. That was all I needed tonight. Raindrops hit the windscreen as I turned into my driveway, and I laughed.

CHAPTER 3

MY PHONE SAT beside me on the bed. Every time a message came in, my heart raced as I checked to see if it was Marc. I growled and lowered the notepad to my lap. The assignment had gone nowhere in an hour. Every time I looked at the notepad instead of seeing the words, I saw Marc's hand writing the notes, and I watched as the ink appeared where his hand had been.

Ding. My finger tingled as I reached out for my phone. I glanced down at the dark screen. My tongue licked my lips. I tapped the home button, and I saw an unknown number with a brief message.

Meet at the public library in 30?

I grabbed my things, muttered a goodbye to my dad, who sat watching footy with two of my brothers, and headed out of the door. Out the front in my car, I smiled at my reflection in the rear-view mirror and let out a laugh.

This is a good sign... hopefully. He could have ignored me if not interested, right?

I made the drive to the library in less than fifteen minutes. Then I checked my watch every minute. *Maybe I was too keen to get here. Maybe it wasn't Marc, after all. Oh, don't tell me this is a setup.* I glanced around and looked for side glances or sneaky conversations.

"Belle?"

I yelped. I didn't mean to; it just happened. My hand reached up to rest on my chest as my heart pounded within it.

"Sorry, I didn't…"

"No, you're fine. My mind was otherwise occupied," I said and waved off the attempted apology.

"Well, I don't think the pelican did it."

My mouth grew dry. *Pelican? What was he…* I turned in the direction he had looked and saw the pelican on the poster. It was one of those posters that were supposed to deter people defacing books in a humorous way; kids thought they were funny at least. I sighed and shook my head.

"Going to defend him, huh? He's got ink on his wings, but then again, it's probably difficult enough for him to turn the pages. Yeah, I'm not sure he could go all out with a pen to have done that kind of damage."

Marc's lips parted before they turned into a smile. He sat down beside me, not across from me, not on the end of the table, he chose the seat beside me. He pulled the seat closer to the table. I felt his jacket brush against my bare arm. I tried to ignore the goosebumps that appeared and opened the notebook that sat on the table.

I waited as Marc adjusted his position in the chair. Muffled music hung in the air from the kid with the ear-buds at the end of the table that bobbed his head back and forth, reminding me we weren't alone. Marc reached out and turned the page.

"Didn't get very far last night then."

A smile crept onto my face and raised my hand to cover it. "I tried."

"Yeah, me too. Wanna see how far I got?"

I nodded. He pulled a small notebook from the pocket of his jacket. Marc flicked the cover up, and I saw a fresh page of lines.

"At least we're consistent," I said.

Marc's fingers left the page and encircled my wrist. He gently tugged my hand away from my mouth. The touch sent the same vibration through my body and I took in a long breath. His fingers unwrapped. I saw them move towards my face. I closed my eyes and kept them shut until I felt the warmth of his touch caress my face.

"We need to get this out of the way, or we won't get anything done today," he whispered into my ear.

I turned my head towards him and opened my eyes. His bright blue eyes stared at me and he moved closer. The room fell silent around as me as his lips touched mine. My hand grabbed his wrist that still held the side of my face, my other hand rested on his shoulder. His hair brushed against the back of my hand as he moved closer. I turned my body towards him and felt his arm around my waist. There seemed to be no string, no pull, but I felt a charged connection. The moment etched itself into my soul and when his lips left mine, I savoured the feeling.

"I've waited four years to do that," he murmured as his forehead rested against mine.

"Four years?" I thought back, that would have been when we first met. "Why didn't you...?"

"Complicated life, remember? I thought it was easier to avoid you." His lips left an invisible impression on my cheek. "I regret not taking you to the formal. I watched for you."

My lips pressed together. "I couldn't bring myself to go."

"I wish you had. If you had, I think I would have caved then. I should have said yes."

"Can't change the past," I replied.

"I just wanted you to know. I wanted to say yes."

My eyelids opened to see his intense gaze. I had sat in the car that night. As far as my family knew, I had gone off to the social, dressed up in a gown I'd only worn once. A photo even sat on the wall in the lounge room with me, smiling. I blinked back the memory and the tears.

"I'm sorry, Belle."

I shook my head. "The past."

My hand slid up his jacket and I gripped the collar. I pulled him back to me and felt his lips on mine again. I didn't know how we remained like that, but when we finally parted, the kid at the end of the table had left.

"Let's get this assignment out of the way."

He nodded in agreement, and we got to work. It didn't seem like we were there for four hours, but the clock didn't lie. We'd used one of the library's computers to type up the assignment before Marc emailed us both a copy. I felt relief seeing the thumbs up on the screen.

"We make a good team," Marc said as we stood outside the library.

"We do."

I reached out and grabbed his hand as we walked down the steps.

"You think we'll ace it?" he asked.

"Course we will. We made sensible arguments with legitimate sources and included references to three of his books. I mean, he can hardly fail us for that, right?"

"Right."

"Belle…"

"Here comes the girls! Fancy meeting you both again so soon," a voice yelled.

Marc had paused on the sidewalk and I saw the source of the statement. I groaned when I saw Jacob crossing the quiet road. He looked the same as he did on the previous encounter; cocky, arrogant... still an idiot.

"Belle, Belle, surely you can do better." Jacob clucked his tongue. "I mean, look at you. You've really... blossomed since last year."

"Shove it Jacob, I'm not interested."

"Well, people can change their mind, he certainly has. Marc was the guy that turned her down for the formal."

Jacob had asked me to the formal. He'd made it a point to tell me at the time how he'd heard how Marc had said no. My body shivered at the thought.

"We settled this the other night Jacob, leave us be," Marc said. He turned to me, "Come on, Belle."

"Woah, not so fast, Marc. I don't know what you did to my mate and I the other night, but it certainly isn't over in my books. Your brother still owes me for a slashed tyre."

"I told you before, if you have an issue with Tim, then take it up with him." Marc's grip tightened on my hand.

"And why would I bother when I have his big brother here? You wouldn't want your brother getting hurt, now, would you? You always came to his rescue, though you were never much of a fighter." Jacob cracked his knuckles and stared at Marc. "I'm ready for round two. We can take it over there."

Something scratched against my arm. I diverted my attention and saw a blue slimmer from beneath the cuff of Marc's jacket. The glow spread to his hand. I could see it was more than a change of colour. The scales, smoothed edged, covered his hand.

"Marc." I moved to the side of him to conceal his hand. "Let it go."

He stepped backwards and his grip eased. His gaze remained on Jacob though, and his clenched jaw only intensified his stare.

"Not today, Jacob, not here. You go find Tim yourself," Marc said.

"One-fifty, Marc." Jacob raised his hand and admired his fist. "One-fifty today or I double it."

"Go ahead," Marc replied.

My free hand moved to cover the scales that were still on his hand and I pushed at him to keep walking. He resisted for a moment before I felt him relent.

"I might not know where you and Tim live, but I know where she does."

"You don't go near Belle," Marc replied.

Marc's hand tensed. I felt a different type of connection between us, just as strong, but cautious... afraid.

"You gotta let it go. Let it go, Marc. Don't think of Jacob. He won't come near me. My brothers can be useless sometimes, but they'd hand him his arse. Come on, Marc." I tugged at Marc's hand and he looked down at me and exhaled.

"What no defence?" Jacob called out.

"Hey, back off or you might find four guys on your doorstep when you least expect it." I bit my tongue. So much for being calm.

"See, that I believe. Okay, I'm not unreasonable. I'll give you a few days to pay up."

Marc and I turned our backs on Jacob and we started towards the busier street ahead with shops.

"A few days. After that, I'm gonna find you or your brother and it won't be for the money. You can count on it!"

"Yeah, good luck with that, mate," Marc muttered.

I glanced over my shoulder long enough to see that Jacob remained on the sidewalk behind us. I leaned my head against Marc's shoulder. We turned the corner and Marc pulled me over to the side and stood in front of me. He released my hand and raised them. They looked perfectly normal now.

"You okay?" I asked.

"Yeah, I think so. Thanks, Belle."

I put my hand on his shoulder. "You would've been able to do that without me."

Marc shook his head and flexed his fingers. "I'm not so confident about that. You saw it, didn't you?"

"Glimpses. Suspicions with no actual answers."

Marc lifted his head to the sky and closed his eyes. "I feel like I'm a damn glow-in-the-dark toy."

I shrugged. "At least it's a gorgeous colour; it matches your eyes."

His warm laughter vibrated through his body as his gaze found mine again. "You're not afraid? You don't think I'm a freak?"

Marc asked and his hand reached out towards me.

The bond tugged at me again. "No, but one day I would like an explanation. At the moment, though, I'm hungry."

"Sounds like a date."

My smile widened as we headed off down the street in search of food.

CHAPTER 4

WE STOPPED OUTSIDE a pizza place and we only had to look at each to know we'd arrived. The aroma of dough baking stirred my empty stomach; I breathed it in. I felt at ease until we got to the counter to order. As much as I hated to admit it, I was a picky eater which made ordering to share tricky. Still, as Marc stood beside me, I felt content enough that he could have ordered pizza with pineapple and I wouldn't have complained.

"What would you like?" Marc asked.

I glanced over at the waitress who stood nearby making a pizza. *To express my opinion or not to, that was the question.* My eyes glanced at the order board. There were a couple there I would eat... with a few slight adjustments.

"Um..." My fingers tapped against my jeans. "I'm really..."

"Tell you what, you order what you like, really. I'm not fussed. I'll go grab a table."

He grabbed my hand. I felt the string tug at my heart. I watched as he turned my hand over and placed a note in it before he closed my fingers around it.

"You sure?" I asked, but he waved his hand as he headed towards a vacant table. When I turned back, the waitress stood there with a smile on her face. "Nice catch. What would you like?"

I placed the order for a chicken pizza, making sure the capsicum, onion, and diced tomato was removed, but I added mushrooms so it wasn't like the pizza would be completely bald when it arrived. The two drinks I'd ordered landed on the counter with the receipt. I hoped he liked cider as I hadn't asked.

"Here, there wasn't much change," I said as I placed the cans on the table. I waited for his hand, but it didn't appear. "Marc, your change."

"Huh?" He looked up at me with those blue eyes. I wanted to reach out and run my hand through his hair. I wanted to know if that silver glow was real or imagined.

"Oh, your change."

53

A coin slipped from my grasp. Marc caught it before it hit the table, despite that he hadn't moved his gaze from me. I fumbled with the remaining coins in my hand and dropped it into his.

"Ta."

I smiled before I sunk into the seat opposite him. Around us, others sat at tables eating, chatting, and playing with their phones. I felt no desire to pull out my phone unless it was to snap a selfie of us together, but that could wait. It would sure beat mooning over his photo in the yearbooks from school.

"There's so much I want to share with someone, with you specifically. I don't know, it probably sounds stupid, but I always thought if there was someone I could tell, it would probably be you. Why, though? I don't know."

"Maybe because you thought I'd listen?"

He shook his head and his hair had a life of its own for a moment before it settled back into place. "No, not that and not here, but I will explain it properly, all of it."

I relaxed into my chair as the pizza arrived on the table. If I had been alone, I probably would have devoured the whole thing, but I tried to appear lady-like and took one slice.

"Not bad," Marc said.

He'd already finished a piece. *Huh, so much for being normal.* I finished that slice of pizza in record time and reached for another.

"You know…" Marc began.

A shadow fell over the pizza and I looked up to see Tim. A vein near his eye pulsed as his gaze alternated between me and Marc. I squirmed in my seat, my shoulders twitched, my foot tapped against the floor.

"Tim," Marc said between bites.

"What's going on?" Tim asked.

I swallowed the mouthful of pizza that scratched at my throat as it went down. My hand reached for the can to wash it down.

"Now's not the time," Marc said and sat back in the seat.

"You know better than to be doing this." Tim jerked his thumb at me without bothering to face me.

"We're celebrating, Tim..."

"I don't care how you want to justify it. Come on, you shouldn't be here. We'll be gone soon."

I watched as Marc looked over at me. Tim's words echoed in my mind.

"When we get home, come on..." Marc started.

Tim grabbed his arm and pulled him up to his feet. Marc's hand reached up into the air, openhanded, and he shook his head.

"It's been a long day, Tim."

"Yeah, I know. I've been texting you for the past few hours and you didn't bother responding once. You know how worried we were."

"Hey, take it outside," the waitress who had served me yelled from behind the counter.

Tim pushed Marc away as he released his grip on Marc's jacket. Marc pulled the jacket down and turned to me.

"I'll be back."

Still, as I watched as they walked into the shop, that string pulled. I turned back to the pizza. It didn't seem as appetising now Marc had left. I glanced back through the shop's window and saw them cross the road and head to the park. Tim flailed his hands at Marc, who batted them away.

I grabbed my jacket and left the stares of the patrons behind. The air felt chilly against my skin as the door closed behind me. I hurried to cross the road and catch up with them as they continued to argue as they moved down the road.

"You shouldn't have even thought about it!" Tim said.

"It's my life. I'm older than you and even if I wasn't, you don't get to tell me what to do."

"This is what we've waited for, Marc. For nineteen years, we've hung on what Mum has said. Are you really going to blow this chance to go back home? To meet our father? I mean, she's just some stupid girl you knew in school."

"You don't understand, Tim, it's more than that."

"Really? You want me to believe that in a matter of days you've fallen in love with some nobody? That you're willing to throw it all away on a stupid crush?"

I slowed down and kept to the shadows of the nearest tree. They weren't far from me, standing opposite each other. Tim's short hair was unwavering while Marc's caressed his face.

"It's not a crush. I don't think it's even been a crush."

"Marc, grow up."

"I've been trying to do that my whole life! I've been trying to decide, to do what I think is right, and every time I do that you or Mum is there to tell me I'm wrong!"

"Because you're not thinking with your brain, idiot."

"According to you," Marc countered.

Tim stepped forward and reached out for Marc's arm again. Marc hit the hand away.

"Leave me alone."

"You really think she would accept you if she knew?" Tim said.

He turned to look in my direction and I moved behind the tree trunk. I glanced around; the shadows were dark enough that he couldn't possibly know I was there, *could he?*

"I think it's up to Belle to make that decision."

"Really?"

Tim took a step back, then his fist connected with Marc's face. Marc stumbled backwards; his hand rubbed his jaw. He looked up at Tim in time to see a right hook headed his way. Marc's eyes glowed blue as his arm raised in defence. He pushed Tim away.

"Really? That's all you've got, brother?" Tim said.

"I don't want to fight you."

"You need to learn to fight for something, so come on."

Tim's eyes glowed blue. I crept around the trunk, careful to remain in the darkest of shadows. His foot connected with Marc's arm, but he didn't go down. Another fist headed to Marc and the blue glow spread. I saw it on Marc's knuckles. Tim sneered as he looked down at Marc crouched on the ground.

"You can't even control that part of you. Even I can do that. It's not the right world for you, Marc. You need to be amongst your own kind."

Marc looked up at Tim, the light blue glow surrounded all his exposed skin. "My own kind? You really think the other world is full of our own kind? That's the problem Tim, we don't belong in either world; we're mixed blood."

"So, you'd choose some girl over your family?"

"I want to choose for myself, whatever it is I do."

"And you can't even do that, can you? You're too scared to tell Mum, too scared to tell Belle. You're just scared."

Marc's leg swung out and connected with the back of Tim's knee. Tim fell to the ground as Marc scrambled over to pin him down with his own body. I saw the wings emerge from his back. His body morphed from human to... to dragon.

"Marc." I thought I whispered it, but the dragon's head turned towards me and then back to Tim.

Tim wiggled his arms, but they remained on the ground. Marc's front claws tightened around Tim's biceps while his legs pinned Tim's knees. His snout moved close to Tim's face, breathing a stream of smoke into Tim's face.

I turned and saw that the streets were quiet, but still, anyone could see Marc in that form and I didn't doubt the problems that could cause.

Urgh, what have you gotten yourself into, Belle? I moved out of the shadows and rushed towards Marc. My shoes skidded on the mud and I felt myself collide with scales.

"Marc, you can't here. Someone could see you."

Smoke puffed from his nostrils but he stepped off Tim, who rolled over. He pushed himself to his feet and rubbed his left arm between the shredded pieces of his shirt.

"You still think you know Marc? You could never know us. You could never understand us. Oh, and don't tell anyone. At least not for a week. After that it won't matter."

"Leave her be, Tim," Marc said, and I turned to see the blue glow die down as his body contorted back into human form.

"Marc…" I reached out to touch his arm, and he moved away.

"You see him now, Belle. He's a danger to himself and everyone else. Walk away." Tim blew a kiss and a snide smile appeared. "Go home Belle. Forget what you've seen."

"I'll make my own decision, thank you," I said and stared at him. Tim heaved a sigh and walked away. I spun around to face Marc. "Marc…"

He remained crouched as I stepped towards him, his head bowed down.

"I'm not afraid of you, Marc."

His shoulders shook, and he reached out his hand to the ground. "It's not that simple, Belle. Tim can, but I can't. I'm afraid of hurting others."

I crouched down in front of him, ran my fingers through his hair to push it aside, and touched his face. His eyes were closed, but I saw the trails that streaked his face. His bottom lip quivered.

"There are many ways to hurt others, including yourself. Tell me what's going on, what's happening in a week."

Marc raised his face. I saw the familiar blue eyes stare back at me through tears. Now wasn't the time to push. I listened to the insistent pull and reached out and wrapped my arms around him.

CHAPTER 5

THE MESSAGES FLASHED past as I checked them again. Still nothing. I dropped the phone onto my bed and wiggled backwards until I felt the wall. Across the room, my reflection looked accurate to how I felt. My mind had spent all night going over what I'd seen, reminding myself it had been real. Still, I didn't have any answers. What I did have were black marks under my eyes that would challenge a panda.

Marc had been so quiet on the drive back to his place I didn't ask about the week, but that hadn't stopped my mind from thinking up hundreds of possibilities. I had tossed and turned. Eventually I'd fallen asleep but I suspected it had only been a few minutes before my alarm went off to remind me that I had a shift at the café.

The phone sat silent and yet it compelled me to pick it up again. I pressed it on and entered my passcode. Once the messages loaded, I tapped against the edge of my phone. I bit my lip as I tried out different messages in my head.

Heading to the café for work. Catch up later?

I clicked the send before I could change my mind and headed to the shower. *Why is the phone so necessary?* It sat there begging for my attention again as I entered the room.

I used my pinkie to bring the screen alive, but only the date and time stared up at me - that and the dragon wallpaper I had installed on the lock screen.

I dressed, brushed out my hair and tied it up without picking up the phone again. Nothing. The damn screen remained in darkness. I scowled at it as I swiped my car keys from my desk and it grabbed it from the bed.

Two hours later, my feet ached. Usually, my face ached first. It was tough smiling so much for customers, but I needed the money and no one hires a grumpy waitress—at least not that I've found yet. I gave the table a final wipe and heard the door buzzer announce a new customer.

My smile faltered as I saw who stood there. *Perhaps it's a coincidence?*

"Tim, what would you like?" I wiped the top of the nearest chair as he walked over.

He waited to speak until he stood close to me. "We need to talk."

"I'm working."

"Your shift ends soon."

My hand paused. I gripped the damp cloth. "Have you been reading my messages?"

"I've done what I need to."

"Belle, just finish up that last table and you're done for the day," my boss called from somewhere behind the counter.

"Thanks, Mrs Henley."

I waved Tim to the side and stacked the cups before moving them to the counter. He didn't say a word while I wiped down the table, straightened the condiments, pushed the chairs back into place, and then shifted the cups to the dishwasher.

Out the back, I untied the apron. If my brothers were any use, I could have summoned them to my defence, but they were probably too busy with their computer games and footy. I could slip out of the back. That would be the easy choice, but then it would annoy me not knowing what he wanted. Urgh, I never had been skilled at walking away. My hand reached up and grabbed my bag. I dug around, found the phone, and called it to life; no reply.

"Shit."

The phone went into the bag and I returned to the front of the café where he waited. I decided to use his tactic and not say a word as I walked past him, but I could hear his footsteps behind me.

"Okay then, speak and then go," I said and crossed my arms in front of me.

"You don't like me much, do you?"

"For some reason, whenever I get near your brother, you're there to interfere. Like in school, like last night, and I suspect it's why you're here now."

"Come on, let's walk and talk. It looks less like we hate each other," Tim said and started walking.

"Why hide the truth?" I muttered before I fell into step with him.

"I know you think I'm being a brat. I can sense you hate me."

"That a dragon power, then?"

I watched as his mouth twitched. He shoved his hands into his pockets as we crossed the road and continued down the road.

"I know you think you like Marc, but I'm not being an arse just to annoy you," he paused. "I'm actually trying to help you."

"Oh, please."

"Hear me out, Belle. I know Marc hasn't told you this yet, so I'm going to give you the non-sugar-coated version."

"Next week it's Marc's birthday. He's nineteen, and that means we can go home. He'll have the power to open the portal from this world to the dragon realm."

My feet paused. "Dragon realm?"

My bag swung as Tim moved to stand in front of me. He glanced around and I did the same. He freed his hand, grabbed my arm and directed me across the road to the font of a closed shop where we were alone.

"My mum stumbled into the dragon realm when the portal hadn't quite closed. The dragons there can shift into human form, but the mix they have isn't the same as what Marc and I have for DNA. Mum fell in love and then along came Marc. After a while, it was clear that he couldn't stay in the realm. Mum says he struggled to breathe and so they opened the portal and sent her through to come back later. Then a few months later, she found out she was carrying me."

"So, you and Marc are half human from this world, but other dragons have another type of human half?"

"Essentially, I think."

"So why didn't your father just come through to this world? Then he could have opened up the portal whenever."

"I don't know. I've asked Mum about that a lot over the years. Look, I've watched her cry over being away from him. She is like a shell of a person here, just waiting to reconnect with him."

"But I'm not her."

"Belle, this has been the plan. We've always known we weren't staying here. Marc will open the portal for us to return, and who knows what will happen. He might have to wait another nineteen years before he can open the portal again. We don't know. You can't put your life on hold when there's no guarantee he'll come back."

"But there are no guarantees in life. What if Marc doesn't want to go? Have you ever considered that maybe he wants to make a life here?"

"We don't belong here."

"Says you," I countered.

"What, you see people shift into dragons all the time, do you?"

"You're defining home as where *you* want to be. You want to go through that portal, you want to see it all, but maybe Marc wants something else."

"You think he doesn't want to meet our dad?"

"I think that blood doesn't make a family."

Tim stepped backwards. "You would take this away from him."

76

"I'm not taking anything. If Marc wants to go, I wouldn't stop him. If Marc wants to stay then I wouldn't think badly of him."

"And what if you two don't work out? What would Marc have then? I'll tell you what: absolutely nothing."

"He can't live his life scared that things will go wrong. Why can't you just let him make that decision? Why can't you just support him? Isn't that what *family* is supposed to do?"

"Family is also about making tough decisions. There's a greater good. How do you think our father will feel if Mum and I arrive without Marc?"

"I don't know."

"Leave him be, Belle. Before you came back into his life, he was set to come with us.

If you do really care for him at all, then you'll let him go. You don't belong with him."

Tim turned and walked away. I tried to think of something to say, but knew it wouldn't make a scrap of difference. I hated when people heaped that kind of guilt onto me. When Tim turned the corner, I felt my phone vibrate.

"What now?" I grumbled.

With the phone retrieved I flicked the screen on. A lone message.

Meet me at the library when you're free.

I looked up at the sky. The library was only a block away, so I headed there on foot.

****

I HAD BEEN around the library at least nine times. If Marc was there then he clearly had some kind of invisibility power. The message had come from his phone, but maybe it hadn't been him at all. Maybe this was Tim trying to prove some unknown point.

Here, can't find you.

Chairs scrapped on the wooden floor near the computers. None of those responsible were Marc. I browsed the shelves closest, but sports explained in excruciating detail didn't capture my undivided attention. This felt horribly like high school. Waiting outside doors I knew he'd exit so I could attempt to strike up a conversation. Signing up as a volunteer when I knew he had as well.

The phone remained silent as I stalked across the library and out the front door. I checked my watch; I'd been there over an hour. My heart sank. I couldn't feel that string pulling me so my feet guided me back to my car. I stared at the empty park.

"I was sure I parked it here." I stepped back from the curb to assess the street. My little car couldn't hide that well. "Oh, come on, seriously. Where's the key?"

My hand felt around the bag. The phone, a few plasters for emergencies, a pen, random receipts I needed to get rid of. I crouched down and set the bag on the sidewalk. Still nothing. I picked it up and watched all the stuff become weird sidewalk art. Nothing. I even felt around the empty bag.

"What the hell? Where are my keys?" I shoved my stuff back into my bag, but held onto the phone. "Shit."

CHAPTER 6

I WALKED OUT of the police station a couple of days later with enough paperwork that at least two trees had died for it. When I looked up, my car sat before me in the street as an officer approached with the key in his hand.

"Thanks," I mumbled.

"Just don't go leaving your key in the car. You're really lucky it's not a burnt-out shell."

That had to be the tenth time an officer had mentioned that. I knew for a fact I hadn't left the key in the car. I had locked the car. Those keys had been in the bag. Lucky, my arse.

I had sent a message each day for three days to Marc, nothing. He hadn't been in class earlier, either. I didn't like to be ghosted. My instinct told me to go to his house and talk to him, but the thought of having to deal with Tim, or worse, Tim and his mum, had put me off until now.

The afternoon sun beat down on my exposed skin, but at least I had my car back in one piece. I sat in the driver's seat and rolled my eyes. Reaching under the seat, I pulled the lever and moved the seat back into its spot.

I tapped the steering wheel, eyed the phone, and decided. With the car in gear, I headed for Marc's place. I needed answers from him.

My confidence grew until I parked the car outside the apartment building. With a turn of the key, the car stilled and I debated the best approach. A direct knock on the door or the indirect beep of a horn. *I probably should knock.*

I pressed against the steering wheel and gave the horn a short blast. When I glanced around the street, I was relieved to see no one glaring at me for the gesture and my gaze fell back to the door. I tried again. The curtain moved. My hand went to the key, ready for a quick escape if necessary.

The string connected, and I felt the pull again. My gaze focused on the door as it opened, and Marc stepped outside. He walked to the passenger window and knocked. I pressed the button, and the window lowered.

"Belle."

I didn't like the coldness in his voice. His gaze went everywhere except to me.

"We need to talk."

"Maybe we should let it go. Go back to before, how it should have stayed. Bye, Belle."

Marc moved away from the car and started down the street.

"What? Not likely, mate."

I followed him in my car as he headed around a corner, crossed the road, turned down another corner, and went a few more blocks. I felt like a full-blown stalker. Twice he glanced at the car, but he continued on until he reached a small playground area. I unbuckled and got out of the car. Even in that moment, I locked the damn thing before I ran after him.

"Marc, stop. Marc!"

He did as I asked and turned to face me.

"What happened? I've been messaging you for days. I went to the library like you asked and you didn't show, and now you're acting like I've committed some heinous crime."

"Wait, what? You haven't messaged me."

"I messaged you every day. If you want, I can get my phone to prove it."

Marc reached into his pocket and pulled out his phone. He frowned as he stared at the screen before he passed it over to me. I could see my last message and then nothing from me, but there were dozens of messages he'd sent me.

"That was the last time I got a message. I figured that after that night, I don't know, maybe you thought Tim made sense and agreed with him."

"I never got those messages. I swear I never received them."

I wanted to move closer, but compelled my feet to stay put. I clicked my name on the top and turned the phone back to him.

"That's not my number."

"Huh?" He took the phone from my hand.

"It's not my number. You know Tim came to see me? He told me about the dragon realm."

"I didn't know. He did?" He put the phone back in his pocket. "Now I feel like shit."

"It was for your own good brother," Tim said as he came into my view.

"You had no right to go behind my back like this. How could you mess with things?" Marc replied.

"This isn't just about you. This whole thing is about you and me and Mum." Tim stepped towards Marc, who backed up a bit.

"No, what you did, that's about you, me, and Belle."

I stepped forward. "Look, Tim, at the moment, I think you should go. Marc and I need to talk without your opinion or interference or anything else."

"No, you need to go home. Man, listen for once in your life and do as you're told."

"And why should I let you tell me what to do? You are nothing to me, Tim. Nothing except an interfering old man who needs to mind his own damn business." I paused. "It was you, wasn't it?"

"What?" Tim's face pleaded innocence.

"You took my keys, didn't you?" I pointed at Tim and he raised his hands. "You set that whole thing up, didn't you? The key, the library, stealing my car!"

"Hope you got some proof of those accusations."

"That was my car, Tim!" I said and pivoted to face him.

Tim shook his head. "I called in the location to the station. I even watched it until they arrived."

"You took her car?" Marc asked. He must have stepped closer as I felt the pull grow stronger.

Tim shrugged. "Relax, I needed you to have some headspace from her."

"Headspace? So, you stole her car?"

"I took care of it alright. She has a life too, Marc. What kind of life could she have with you? You're a dragon—she's a human."

"That's her choice, my choice. Our parents made that choice."

"And look at the pain that caused Mum, at least. You really think that it's fair for Belle to go through that? Today is that day Marc. This isn't something that might happen way in the future. It's tomorrow."

"Tomorrow?" I whispered. *No, tomorrow? They were going tomorrow?*

Marc's hand glowed as he raised it. By the time I turned to look at him, he was in dragon form. I stepped away as he stretched out his

89

wings and stepped towards Tim with his head low to the ground.

"Fine, you wanna do it that way?" Tim yelled.

Now there were two dragons. A tree line hopefully would obscure them. Mostly. I took another step backwards as they stalked each other in a circle. My heart raced as I looked to distinguish which one was Marc. They looked almost identical except for colour; one blue shimmered brighter than the other.

Marc launched off the ground. Tim did too. Their claws scratched at each other. Tim's head jerked back as he roared. I saw the blood that ran from a cut on his front leg. Marc kicked out with his hind leg and connected with Tim's stomach. Tim flapped out of reach as Marc circled higher. Tim lashed out with both sets of front claws but found only air.

"Marc! Marc, this is not the way…" My voice seemed so quiet.

The sky darkened as their individual glow set them apart. Marc flew towards Tim, who turned to fly up but changed directions. A claw cut into Marc's front leg. My hand covered my arm as I felt the pain.

When I looked skyward again, they hovered in the air. Their gazes locked on each other. Tim flapped his wings and surged forward. Marc remained still and blue flames flew from his mouth and hit Tim. Engulfed by the flames, Tim's wings drooped as his body fell to the ground.

I ran over to him as he morphed back into human form. His chest moved. His arm still bled. The ground shook as Marc landed a little way off. Beyond him, I saw a woman headed towards us.

"Marc, what have you done?" she cried as she ran past him and to Tim. "Tim, honey? Honey, answer me."

Their mother. The resemblance between her and Tim was unmistakable. She turned to me.

"I didn't do anything," I protested.

"What colour? What colour was the flame?"

I turned my head towards Marc, who remained in dragon form. "Um, it was blue."

"Magic fire, thank goodness. Tim, honey, you're okay..."

Tim muttered something in response, but his eyes remained closed.

I got up and walked towards Marc. His gaze seemed to be on Tim and his mum.

"Marc..."

He shook his head. His wings stretched out, and he bobbed down.

"No wait..."

But he didn't. He turned and flew. Sparks flew from the power line as his leg connected with it. He roared, but didn't stop. I tore my gaze from him and back to his mum.

"You feel it, I can see that. Go after him," she said.

I turned and ran for my car.

CHAPTER 7

IN THE CAR, I looked through the windscreen and searched the night sky. He wasn't much more than a flash of blue, but I felt the pull to him stronger than ever. My eyes fell on the distant mountain. We only had the one on the edge of town but it had a beautiful view of the city. My instinct told me to head there.

The engine roared as I turned the key. My fingers gripped the wheel as the wheels screeched as they searched for contact with the road. The potent smell of rubber permeated the car even with the windows up. I felt the car slide and then it moved.

I tried to focus on the road. Lights from oncoming cars annoyed me as I struggled to stick to the speed limit. The city limit sign appeared, and I pushed my foot down. The road appeared quieter now I had left the city behind me. I took a corner too fast and pressed on the brake. The car swerved but didn't connect to the road barriers.

The blue light vanished from view. I kept Marc at the front of my mind. His face, his touch, his smell. The higher up the mountain I drove, the more impatient I felt. Then I arrived. I turned the car off the road and onto the dirt. I drove between trees and searched for a blue light.

"Where are you, Marc?"

I parked the car and killed the car's lights. I glanced around the trees and bushes and shadows. The shadows here made me uncomfortable. Marc had to be close. I felt the bond.

The breeze moved the leaves, and I rubbed my arms. I should have grabbed a jacket. Trees, bushes, and more trees. More bushes. A groan.

"That's more like it."

I followed the direction I thought it came from. My feet quickened though as the bond pulled tight. Perhaps it knew something I didn't, but whatever the feeling was, I had to trust it.

"Marc, Marc, I know you're out there. Marc, please let me know where you are." A sharp groan drew my attention to the left. I waited but couldn't hear anything except the leaves as the wind demanded they dance.

The bond seemed to waver. I closed my eyes. In my mind I pictured Marc and I felt the connection reignite, hold, and strengthen.

I moved into the shadows of the trees. The bushes were thick, but I pushed through them until they cleared. There on the ground, I saw him hunched over; his arm cradled in his hand.

"Marc? Are you okay Marc?"

Goosebumps covered my arms as I waited for him to reply. He didn't look up or turn towards me.

"This isn't your decision, Belle. This is up to me. I need to decide on all this even though it's already decided. This, this just can't be."

I suspected if it was anyone else, I would've walked away, but not Marc. The bond felt taut between us and it urged me to go to him. I closed the gap and knelt down beside him. My hand reached out and rested on his shoulder. I wished and waited a moment for him to respond, but nothing.

"You do have a choice, Marc. You've always had a choice. Just for a moment, you need to stop thinking about what your mum wants, what Tim wants, and even what I want." I paused and my grip tightened on his shoulder. "Marc, what is it you want?"

"I just want to be happy. I don't know what I want, I don't think. Sure, I want to meet my father and I want to get to know him. I want to know that side of me, but I enjoy living here. I enjoy being on Earth. I want to finish uni. I want to see where life can lead me here."

"There's nothing wrong with that. This is your life, Marc, and nobody else's."

He lifted his head up and his blue eyes glinted in the moonlight. No smile covered his handsome face, just a pain. I released my hold on his shoulder and reached down to take his hand. My finger brushed against the back of it, too close to the wound, and he winced. He raised up his hand, and the moonlight revealed the consequence of his flight.

His leg had a cut from Tim's claws, but it didn't look as bad as the burn. His skin was red raw with black patches.

"From when you hit the wires?" I whispered.

Marc nodded. "Wasn't watching where I was going, was I?"

"I think I might have something in the boot of my car. Come on."

I stood up and waited for Marc to do the same. My hand reached out and grabbed his uninjured hand. He rose from the ground as I stood and followed me. I paused near a tree.

"What's wrong?"

"I don't know where I parked the car."

A smile crossed his face. "It's this way."

"Dragon sense for the win," I replied.

Sure enough, we found my car, and I unlocked it as we approached. Marc dragged his feet as he walked, and I felt his body sway as we neared the car. He seemed relieved to rest against the side of it when we finally reached it.

"Why don't you sit in the back seat or something? And lie down if you're feeling dizzy while I see what I have."

I opened the back door and watched Marc as he sat down, still holding his hand. At the boot, I busied myself trying to find something, anything. The best I came up with was a box of tissues which weren't going to do much for anything - unless I suddenly felt the urge to bawl.

Defeated, I slammed the boot shut. *Stupid*. I stepped around the car to find that Marc had slid into the backseat. He sat there with his eyes closed; his blistered hand in his lap and weeping.

"I think we need to get you to the hospital as I haven't got anything to help with it."

Marc shook his head. "I can't. What if they find out what I am? I don't want to find myself locked away in some little white room as a government experiment."

"I would never let that happen."

His eyes remained closed. Raindrops splattered my bare skin; I slipped into the car and closed the door. To face him, I turned my back on the window.

"I'm so afraid of making the wrong decision. I'm so afraid of hurting someone. You saw that, I hurt Tim. I'm afraid of hurting you. I'm still afraid of hurting you."

"Then stop pushing me away, Marc. Surely you can feel that we are connected. I can't explain what it is, but it's something I've only felt about you, even when we were in high school. Something draws me to you."

Marc's eyes opened, and he turned his head towards me. His eyebrows dipped as he stared at me.

"Like a string that connects us," he said.

That string continued to pull me towards him with a sense of urgency. I stared back at him while my heart pounded. His knee moved and touched mine, and I felt a wave rush through my veins.

Marc raised his uninjured hand; it trailed up my arm and across my shoulder before it found the back of my head. He cupped his hand until it fit snuggly against my neck. I swallowed as the string urged us to connect.

The space between us vanished as he leaned forward. My hand reached up, and I traced down the side of his face with my finger. Marc's lips found mine. I felt the bond between us merge into something complete.

My hand slipped around his neck as my body moved against his.

"Ouch."

Marc pulled away; his eyes squinted as he grimaced. We both turned to look as he raised his injured hand. A blue glow surrounded it and became brighter before it faded away to reveal his hand. I glanced at his leg and saw no cut between the torn denim of his jeans.

"I can't heal," he whispered. He returned his gaze to me. "Maybe it's you."

I smiled. "I'm just a human."

"No, you're much more than that. Your soul speaks with mine, not just for my human side, your soul connects to mine, to all of me. It's what keeps drawing us together. I want you to know all of me, Belle."

"I want to, Marc. I'm not afraid of who you are."

Marc's lips found mine again, and I felt his healed hand reach around my waist. He pulled me to him. His body pressed against mine. I leaned back on the seat as our souls intertwined and our bond forged to the deepest level.

CHAPTER 8

MY FINGERS TAPPED on the steering wheel as I watched the front door. It seemed like hours ago Marc went inside and the light in the window turned on. The brake pedal ascended as my foot relaxed. I checked my watch again.

The window darkened and my gaze moved back to the door of the apartment. My foot bounced against the floor to give my fingers a break.

"Come on, Marc."

The door handle turned, and I saw him exit before he turned to lock the door. I had expected him to look concerned, upset maybe, but...

"They're gone already," he said as he plopped down on the passenger seat.

"Do you know where?"

Marc turned to look at me. "I don't know. Mum never really said where it would all happen, just that it would."

"Anywhere special for your mum, somewhere that you would all go?"

Marc sat back in the seat and turned his attention to the windscreen. My finger tapped again; I closed my eyes and willed myself to calm down.

"On her birthday, she liked to take us to the park near the high school."

"That conservation park?"

"Yeah, that's the one."

"Let's go then."

"But I'm not sure Belle. It's a guess. What if I'm wrong? I don't want them to just leave, not after the last time I saw them."

"Marc..."

"I have to make it right, Belle. I have to make sure that I'm doing something right with everything."

I nodded.

"Can you connect to them? Like with us, but them?"

Marc's head turned towards me. "I don't know. I've never had to, never tried. I don't know how to find it. It's different with you."

"I'm sure you're bonded with them, too. Close your eyes, picture them in your mind, feel that love you have for them, feel how much you want to make this right before they leave."

"Is that how you found me on the mountain?"

I smiled. Marc clenched his jaw and then nodded. He pulled the car door closed and relaxed with his head against the seat. I turned the key, and the engine hummed while I watched him. He looked tense.

"I can't sense them," he growled.

"Relax Marc, put your immediate concerns aside and just think of them."

His mouth opened, and a breath exhaled. He breathed in before he allowed it to slowly leave his lips. His shoulders lowered; his hand released the fabric of his jeans.

"Straight ahead, towards the park," he whispered.

I smiled as I put the car into gear. When I looked again, his attention had landed on me.

"Thanks, Belle."

I followed the road until we turned onto the highway. We both sat in silence as the moon hung high overhead. The park had been a place for my childhood as well, but I'd never been there after dark as the gate got locked on the road by 6pm. At night, the road looked different as bright lights would blind me for a second as they passed me by.

When I saw the roundabout ahead, I flicked the blinker on and we turned left. I glanced at Marc, his attention on where we were going.

"You okay?"

"It feels stronger. It's a different feeling than with you. I don't know how to describe it."

I pulled the car into a park near the closed gate and we exited. The only other car there was a blue one.

"We're in the right spot then," I said and pointed towards the car.

"Yeah, but we still have to find them," Marc replied and grabbed my hand. "Come on, this way."

He led the way as we crossed the car park to the gate and ducked beneath it. We ran down the road towards the walkway that led to a picnic area. My shoes crunched the gravel as we left the road before we thundered over the wooden walkway.

"They can't open it without you, right?" I asked between gasps for air.

"Not that I know of, I don't know. None of us really know the rules with this."

"There they are."

I pointed towards two figures that stood beside each other. They turned towards us as we neared. I could see his mum had been crying. I slowed down and pulled Marc to a stop.

"You should go ahead."

"Not this time, together, Belle."

We walked the rest of the way and his mum stepped forward.

"You're not coming, are you?" she said.

"I can't. There's so much I want to do here. I'm connected to being here." Marc turned to me and grabbed my hand. "I'm connected to people."

"Like a rope that pulls you so tight you think it might break at any moment, but it never does." I looked up at her and she smiled at me. "It was the same when I met their father. You should have told me sooner, Marc."

"I didn't know how. This is what you've talked about our entire lives..."

She raised her hand and nodded. "I was perhaps selfish in that regard. I can't fault you for finding your destined soul and

114

wanting to be with her. We will work on a way to have the portal open again."

"Worst case, it will be next year, on my birthday, when I get the portal power," Tim added and stepped up beside his mum.

"He's right." Their mum pulled Marc into a hug. He let go of my hand and I stepped away. "You keep yourself safe, keep practising control. I love you always."

She moved away before she shoved Tim forward. "Sorry about the..." Tim pointed to where the wound was. "How'd you do that?"

"I didn't," Marc replied. "At least I don't think it was me."

"Your father can heal him in the other realm," their mum said.

"I love you, brother," Tim said.

"I love you too, baby brother. All is forgiven." They embraced, and I heard Marc whisper, "Take care of Mum."

"I will." Tim stepped back and turned to me. He opened his mouth, and I wondered what he would say, but he said nothing. He nodded at me and turned away to his mother.

Marc moved closer to me and caught my hand again. He pulled me close and his arm wrapped around my waist.

"You can still change your mind," I whispered.

I watched as their mum waved her hand. Nothing happened. Marc raised his hand. I watched as a light blue stream of magic left his hand and snaked around his family. It twisted about until it began moving in an anti-clockwise direction. The trees faded

116

from view inside the trail, and Marc's mum looked over her shoulder and smiled.

"We'll see you soon Marc and you too, Belle," she said.

My eyes fixated on the mountains beyond her, though. A dragon flew in the distance in a place where the sun had already risen. A dragon head came into view and puffed smoke. A blue glow surrounded it for a moment before a middle-aged man stood there with his arms outstretched.

His mum turned, and together with Tim, she walked into the portal. The man rushed forward and hugged her before he glanced towards me and Marc.

"I'm proud of you son, I'll see you at the next opening."

The blue light faded and the three of them disappeared. Marc and I stood alone in the deserted park.

"You need anything?" I asked.

Marc wiped his face with his hand. I stepped around and drew him close to me. His other arm wrapped around me and I felt his damp face rest next to mine.

"I have what I need."

"Marc?"

"Yeah?" I pulled away a little.

"No matter where you go, I'll be there too."

"I hope there are some exceptions to that," he said, and smiled. "I mean–"

I smiled. "You know what I mean."

"I do."

His lips moved to mine. I enjoyed the rush of feelings that coursed through my body as his grip tightened and the string that bound us tingled with happiness.

$\mathcal{A}$UTHOR $\mathcal{T}$HANKS

This novelette had a rocky start and sat on my computer for some time before it was included in the *Adamant Spirits: 2022 Charity Anthology*.

Now, it is released on its own. I want to thank Andrea Fodor of CReya-tive for the stunning cover artwork that inspired this story in the first place.

To the *Romantic Fantasy Shelf* co-ordinators who released the anthology and gave this story a chance to help others in need.

And I can't forget my readers. Without you my stories would still be on computer!

FIND OUT MORE

Stay up to date with
my releases on my website

www.jenniwardauthor.com.au

www.ingramcontent.com/pod-product-compliance
Lightning Source LLC
Chambersburg PA
CBHW020530120726
47904CB00003B/1027